S

OUR OLD NURSERY RHYMES

H. Willebeek Le Mair

ILLUSTRATIONS BY
HENRIETTE WILLEBEEK LE MAIR

EDITED BY DAWN AND PETER COPE

GALLERY CHILDREN'S BOOKS
LONDON AND THE HAGUE

THIS VOLUME OF BEAUTIFULLY
ILLUSTRATED NURSERY RHYMES
IS THE WORK OF THE DUTCH ARTIST
HENRIETTE WILLEBEEK LE MAIR (1889-1966).

SHE WAS THE DAUGHTER OF A
WEALTHY MERCHANT WHO HAD AN INTEREST
IN ART AND ENCOURAGED HER TO PAINT AND
DRAW FROM AN EARLY AGE.

PUBLISHERS WERE ATTRACTED BY HER
DELICATE AND DETAILED DRAWINGS AND
HER FEELING FOR DECORATION AND
MISS LE MAIR WAS COMMISSIONED TO
ILLUSTRATE SEVERAL CHILDREN'S BOOKS
WITH RHYMES BETWEEN 1911-1926.

'OUR OLD NURSERY RHYMES', FIRST
PUBLISHED IN 1911, AND ITS COMPANION
VOLUME 'LITTLE SONGS OF LONG AGO',
1912, ARE SURELY THE MOST BEAUTIFUL
SET OF ALL THE BEST-LOVED RHYMES
EVER ILLUSTRATED.

CONTENTS

LITTLE BO-BEEP

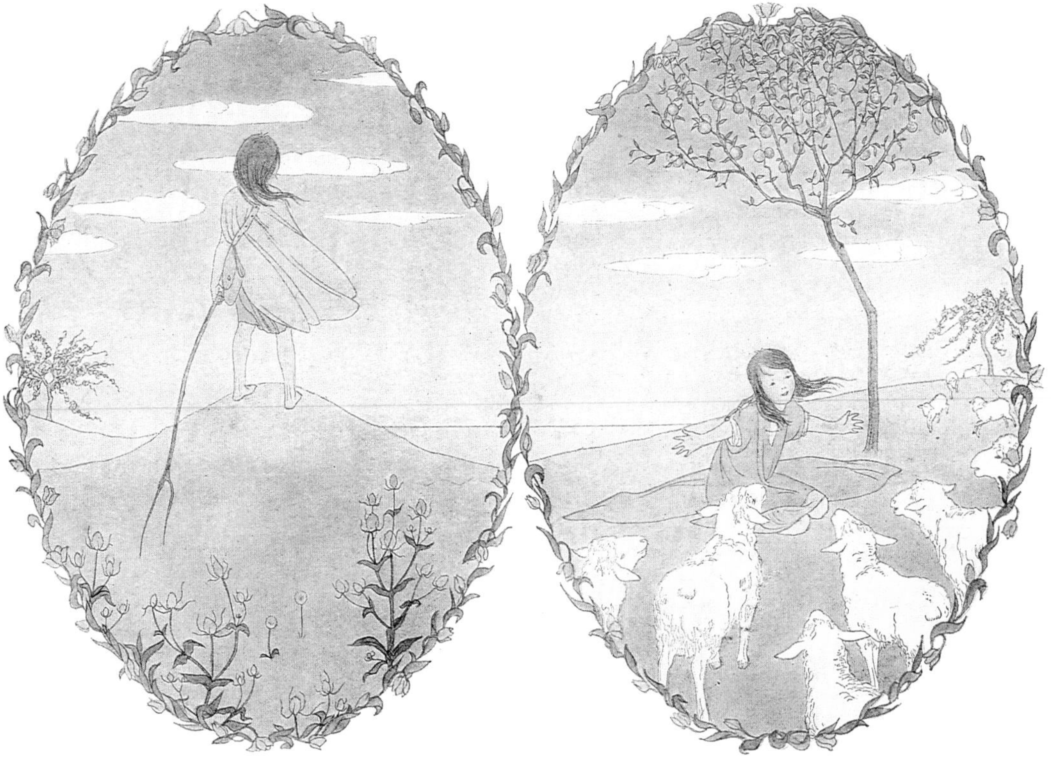

Little Bo-peep has lost her sheep,
And can't tell where to find them;
   Leave them alone
     And they'll come home,
Bringing their tails behind them.

Little Bo-peep fell fast asleep,
And dreamt she heard them bleating;
   But when she awoke,
     She found it a joke,
For they were still a-fleeting.

Then up she took her little crook,
Determined for to find them;
   She found them indeed,
     But it made her heart bleed,
For they'd left their tails behind them.

It happened one day, as Bo-peep did stray
Into a meadow hard by,
   There she espied
     Their tails side by side,
All hung on a tree to dry.

She heaved a sigh, and wiped her eye,
And over the hillocks went rambling.
   And tried what she could,
     As a shepherdess should,
To tack again each to its lambkin.

DANCE A BABY DIDDY

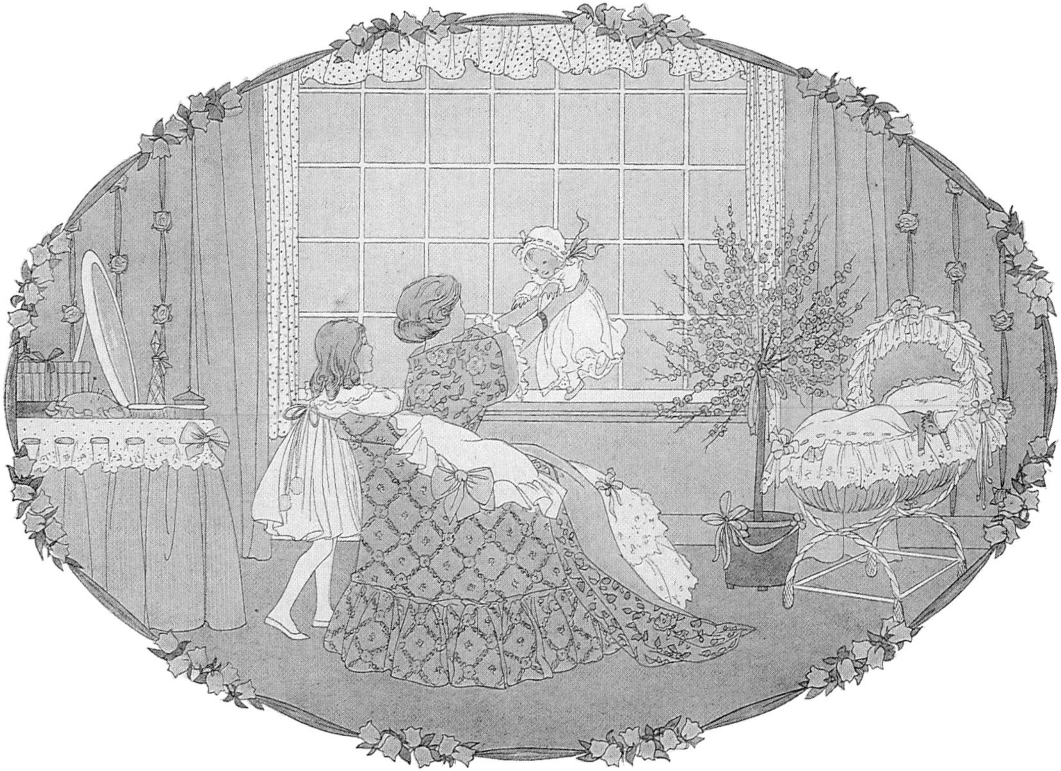

Dance a baby, diddy,
What can mammy do wid' e,
But sit in her lap,
    And give 'un some pap,
And dance a baby diddy?

Mary, Mary, quite contrary,
How does your garden grow?
With silver bells and cockle shells,
And pretty maids all in a row.

WHAT ARE LITTLE BOYS MADE OF?

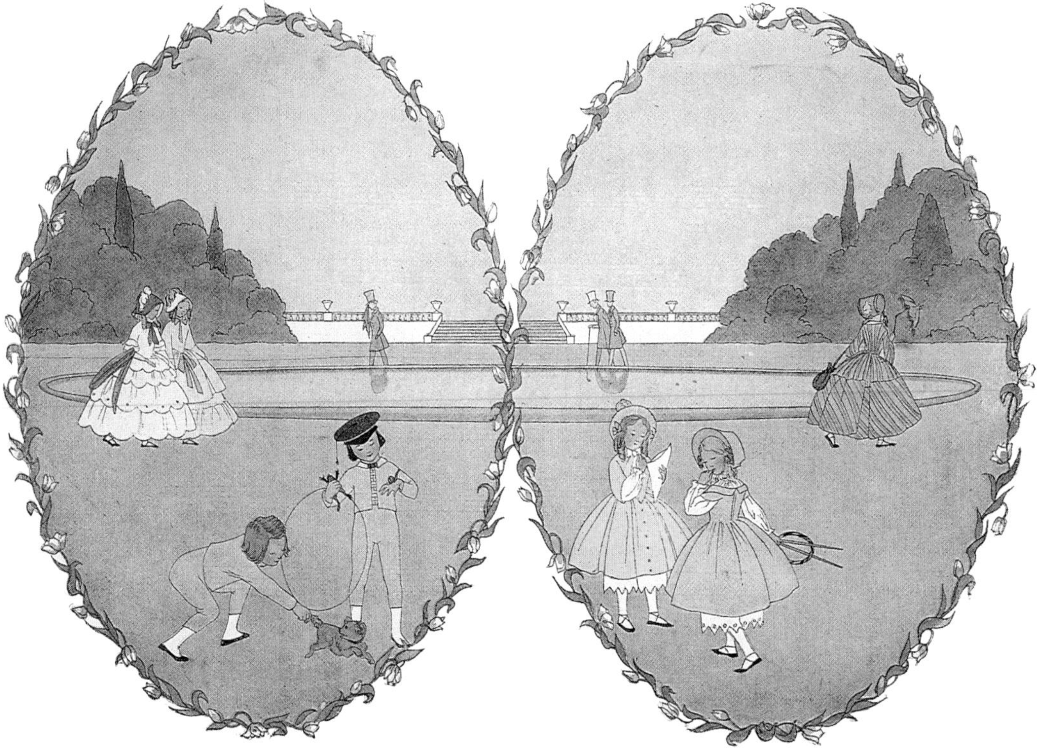

What are little boys made of?
　What are little boys made of?
Frogs and snails and puppy-dogs' tails,
　That's what little boys are made of.

What are little girls made of?
　What are little girls made of?
Sugar and spice and all that's nice,
　That's what little girls are made of.

What are our young men made of?
　What are our young men made of?
Sighs and leers and crocodile tears,
　That's what our young men are made of.

What are young women made of?
　What are young women made of?
Ribbons and laces and sweet pretty faces,
　That's what young women are made of.

Little Jack Horner
Sat in the corner,
Eating a Christmas pie;
He put in his thumb,
And pulled out a plum,
And said, What a good boy am I!

O dear, what can the matter be?
   Dear, dear, what can the matter be?
O dear, what can the matter be?
   Johnny's so long at the fair.

He promised he'd bring me a basket of posies,
   A garland of lilies, a garland of roses,
He promised to bring me a bunch of blue ribbons
   To tie up my bonny brown hair.

I LOVE LITTLE PUSSY

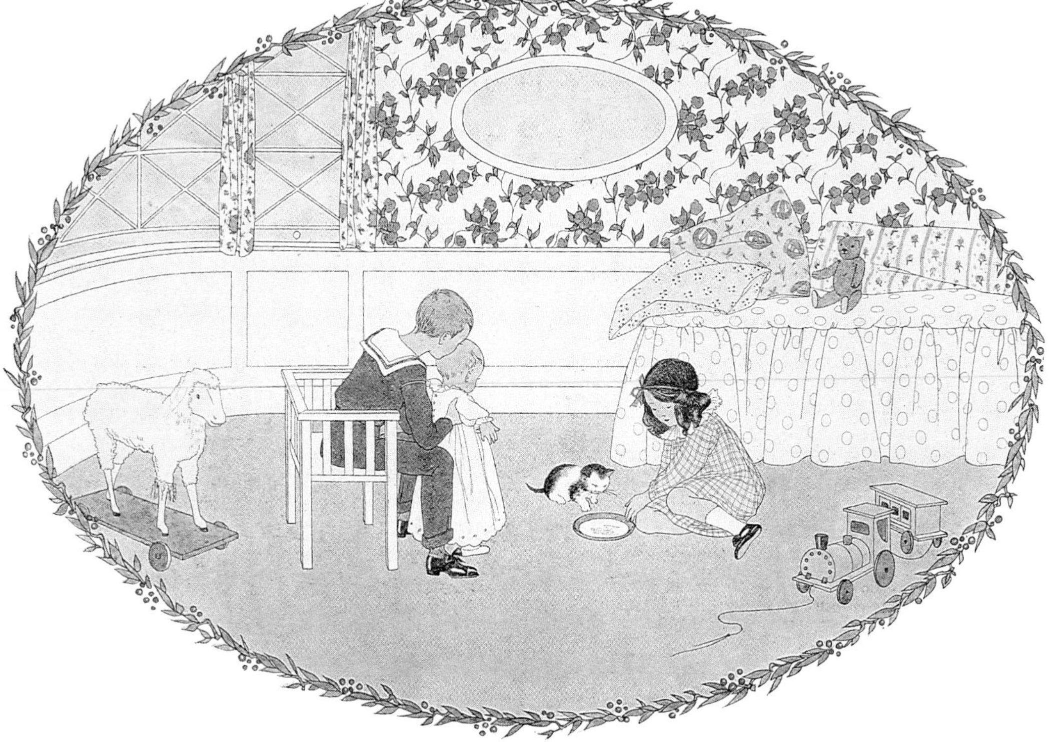

I love little pussy,
  Her coat is so warm,
And if I don't hurt her
    She'll do me no harm.

So I'll not pull her tail,
    Nor drive her away,
But pussy and I
    Very gently will play.

Lucy Locket lost her pocket,
Kitty Fisher found it;
Not a penny was there in it,
Only a ribbon round it.

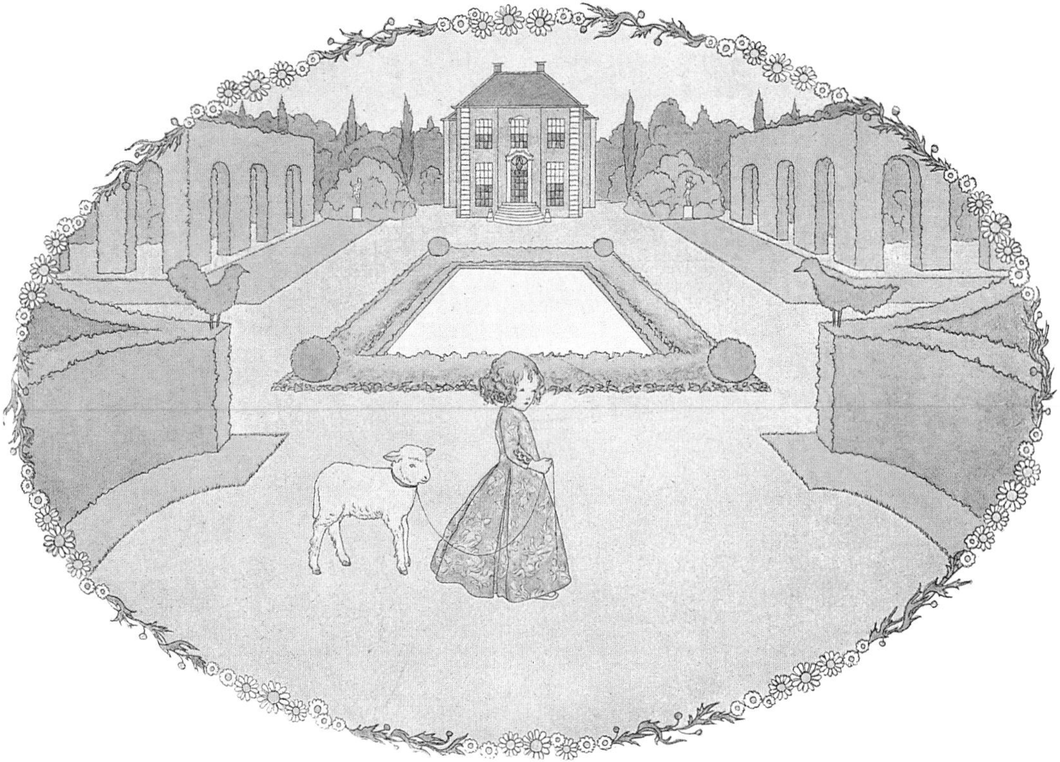

Mary had a little lamb,
It's fleece was white as snow;
And everywhere that Mary went ·
   The lamb was sure to go.

It followed her to school one day,
   That was against the rule;
It made the children laugh and play
   To see a lamb at school.

And so the teacher turned it out,
   But still it lingered near,
And waited patiently about
   Till Mary did appear.

Why does the lamb love Mary so?
   The eager children cry;
Why, Mary loves the lamb, you know,
   The teacher did reply.

Goosey, goosey gander,
Wither shall I wander?
Upstairs and downstairs
   And in my lady's chamber.
There I met an old man
   Who would not say his prayers.
I took him by the left leg
   And threw him down the stairs.

Baa, baa, black sheep,
Have you any wool?
Yes, sir, yes, sir,
   Three bags full;
One for the master,
   And one for the dame,
And one for the little boy
   Who lives down the lane.

Jack and Jill went up the hill
To fetch a pail of water;
Jack fell down and broke his crown,
    And Jill came tumbling after.

Up Jack got, and home did trot,
    As fast as he could caper,
To old Dame Dob, who patched his nob
    With vinegar and brown paper.

Here we go round the Mulberry bush,
The Mulberry bush, the Mulberry bush;
Here we go round the Mulberry bush
  On a cold and frosty morning.

This is the way we wash our hands,
  Wash our hands, wash our hands;
This is the way we wash our hands
  On a cold and frosty morning.

This is the way we dry our hands,
  Dry our hands, dry our hands;
This is the way we dry our hands
  On a cold and frosty morning.

This is the way we clap our hands,
  Clap our hands, clap our hands;
This is the way we clap our hands
  On a cold and frosty morning.

This is the way we warm our hands,
  Warm our hands, warm our hands;
This is the way we warm our hands
  On a cold and frosty morning.

The north wind doth blow,
  And we shall have snow,
And what will poor robin do then?
    Poor thing.
He'll sit in a barn,
    And keep himself warm,
And hide his head under his wing.
    Poor thing.

Little Boy Blue,
Come blow your horn,
The sheep's in the meadow,
    The cow's in the corn;
But where is the boy
    Who looks after the sheep?
He's under a haycock
    Fast asleep.
Will you wake him?
    No, not I,
    For if I do, he's sure to cry.

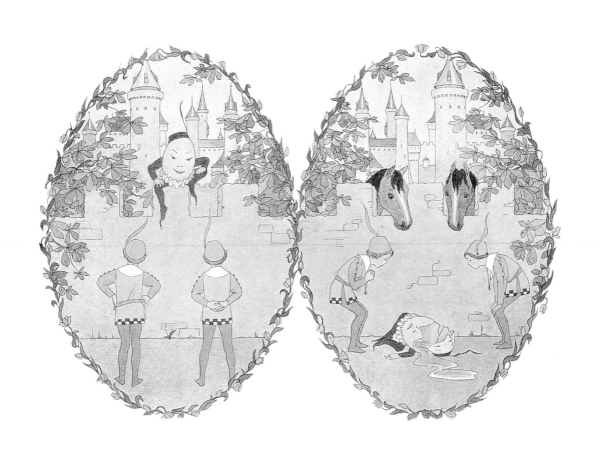

Humpty Dumpty sat on a wall,
Humpty Dumpty had a great fall.
All the king's horses,
    And all the king's men,
Couldn't put Humpty together again.

O where, oh where has my little dog gone?
O where, oh where can he be?
With his ears cut short and his tail cut long,
O where, oh where is he?

Dance to your daddy,
My little babby,
Dance to your daddy,
My little lamb;

You shall have a fishy
In a little dishy,
You shall have a fishy
When the boat comes in.

Yankee doodle came to town,
  Riding on a pony;
He stuck a feather in his cap
  And called it macaroni.
Yankee doodle, doodle do,
  Yankee doodle dandy,
All the lasses are so smart,
  And sweet as sugar candy.

Marching in and marching out,
  And marching round the town, O!
Here there comes a regiment
  With Captain Thomas Brown, O!
Yankee doodle, doodle do,
  Yankee doodle dandy,
All the lasses are so smart,
  And sweet as sugar candy.

Yankee doodle is a tune
  That comes in mighty handy;
The enemy all runs away
  At Yankee doodle dandy.
Yankee doodle, doodle do,
  Yankee doodle dandy,
All the lasses are so smart,
  And sweet as sugar candy.

Three little kittens
  They lost their mittens,
And they began to cry,
    Oh, mother dear, we sadly fear
    That we have lost our mittens.
What! lost your mittens,
You naughty kittens!
    Then you shall have no pie.
    Mee-ow, mee-ow, mee-ow.
No, you shall have no pie.

The three little kittens
They found their mittens,
And they began to cry,
    Oh, mother dear, see here, see hear,
    For we have found our mittens.
Put on your mittens,
You silly kittens,
    And you shall have some pie.
    Purr-r, purr-r, purr-r,
Oh, let us have some pie.

The three little kittens
  Put on their mittens,
    And soon ate up the pie;
    Oh, mother dear, we greatly fear
That we have soiled our mittens.
What! soiled your mittens,
Your naughty kittens!
    Then they began to sigh
    Mee-ow, mee-ow, mee-ow.
Then they began to sigh.

The three little kittens
    They washed their mittens,
And hung them out to dry;
    Oh! mother dear, do you not hear
    That we have washed our mittens?
What! washed your mittens,
Then you're good kittens,
But I smell a rat close by.
    Mee-ow, mee-ow, mee-ow.
    We smell a rat close by.

Three blind mice, see how they run!
They all ran after the farmer's wife,
Who cut off their tails with a carving knife,
Did ever you see such a thing in your life,
As three blind mice?

Young lambs to sell!
Young lambs to sell!
I never would cry
    Young lambs to sell,
If I'd as much money
    As I could tell
I never would cry
    Young lambs to sell.

PUSSY CAT, PUSSY CAT

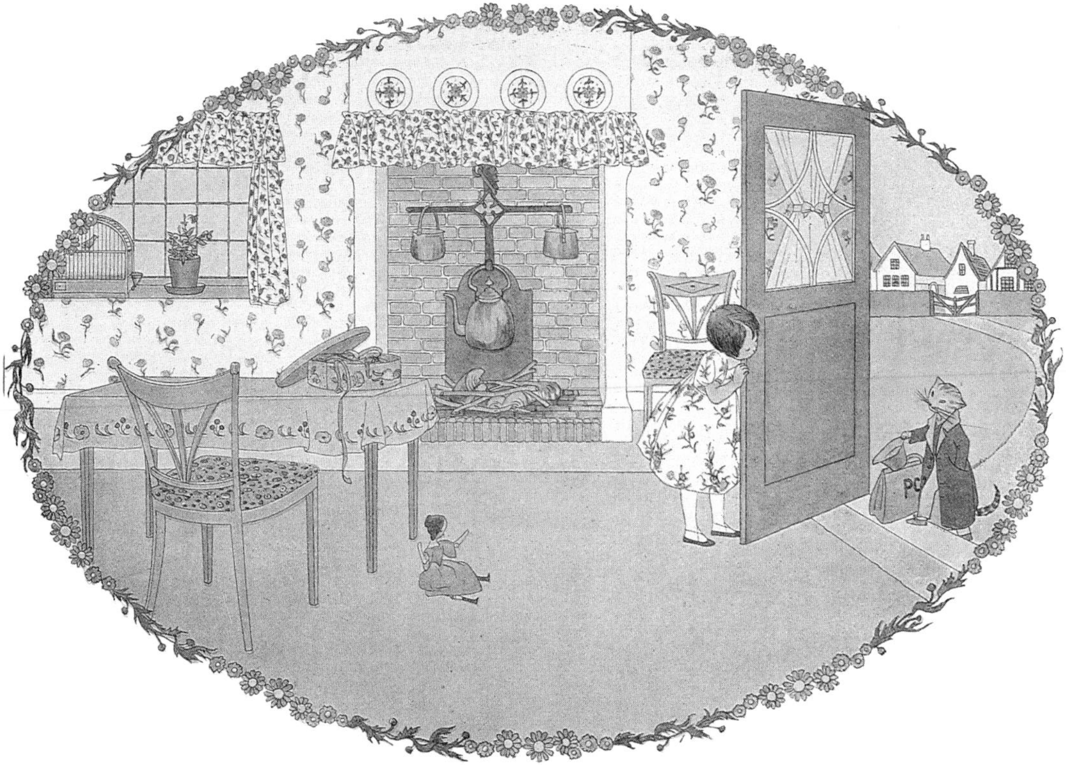

Pussy cat, pussy cat,
 Where have you been?
I've been to London
 To look at the queen.
Pussy cat, pussy cat,
 What did you there?
I frightened a little mouse
 Under her chair.

DING, DONG, BELL

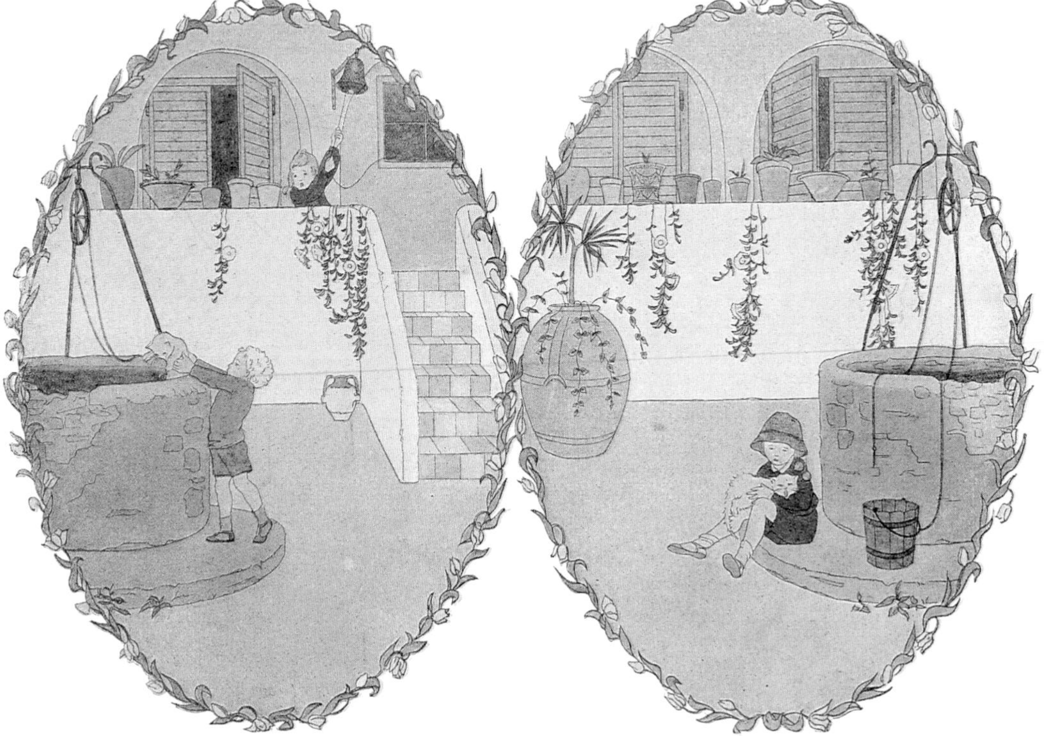

Ding, dong, bell,
Pussy's in the well.
Who put her in?
   Little Johnny Green.
Who pulled her out?
   Little Tommy Stout.
What a naughty boy was that,
   To try to drown poor pussy cat,
Who never did him any harm,
   And killed the mice
   In his father's barn.

Georgie-Porgie, pudding and pie,
Kissed the girls and made them cry;
When the boys came out to play,
  Georgie-Porgie ran away.

R ide a cock-horse
To Banbury Cross,
To see a fine lady
Upon a white horse
Rings on her fingers
And bells on her toes,
And she shall have music
Wherever she goes.

LITTLE MISS MUFFETT

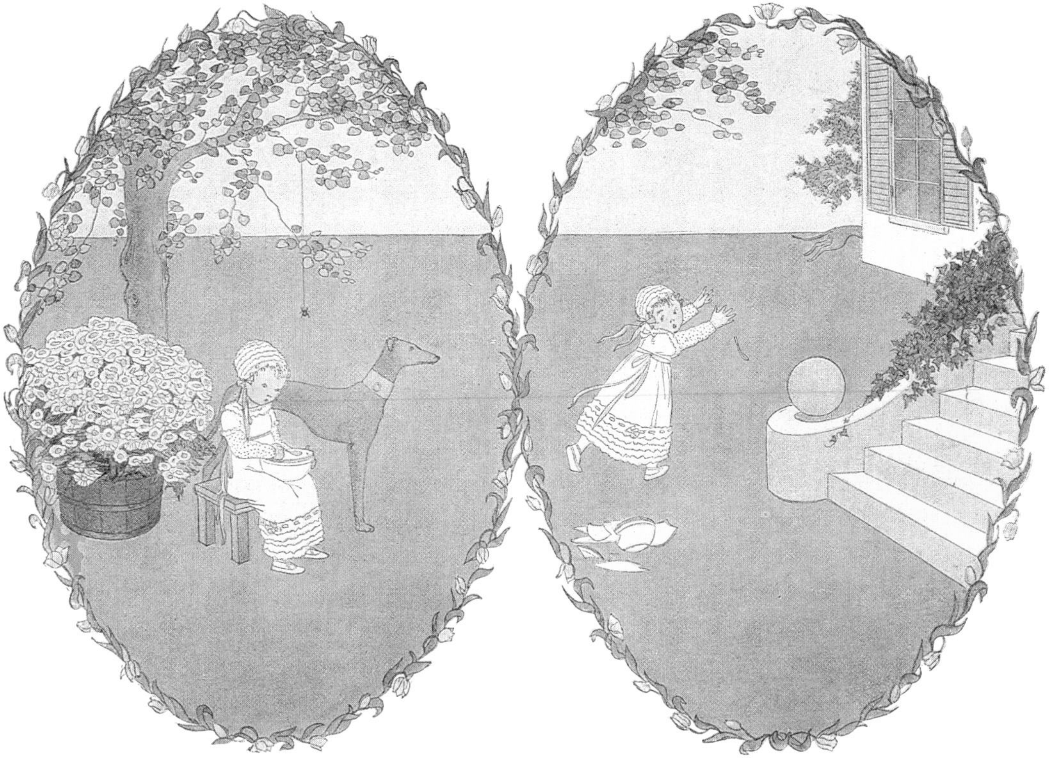

L ittle Miss Muffet
Sat on a tuffet,
Eating her curds and whey;
   There came a big spider,
Who sat down beside her
   And frightened Miss Muffet away.

There was a little man,
And he wooed a little maid,
And he said, Little maid,
Will you wed, wed, wed?
I have little more to say,
Than will you, yea or nay?
For the least said is soonest mended, ded, ded.

The little maid replied,
If I should be your bride,
Pray what must we have
For to eat, eat, eat?
Will the love that you're so rich in
Make a fire in the kitchen,
And the little god of love turn the spit, spit, spit?

Then the little man he sighed,
Some say a little cried,
And his little heart was big
With sorrow, sorrow, sorrow;
I'll be your little slave,
And if the little that I have
Be too little, little dear, I will borrow, borrow, borrow.

Thus did the little gent
Make the little maid relent,
For her little heart began
To beat, beat, beat;
Though his offers were but small,
She accepted of them all.
Now she thanks her little stars for her fate, fate, fate.

POLLY PUT THE KETTLE ON

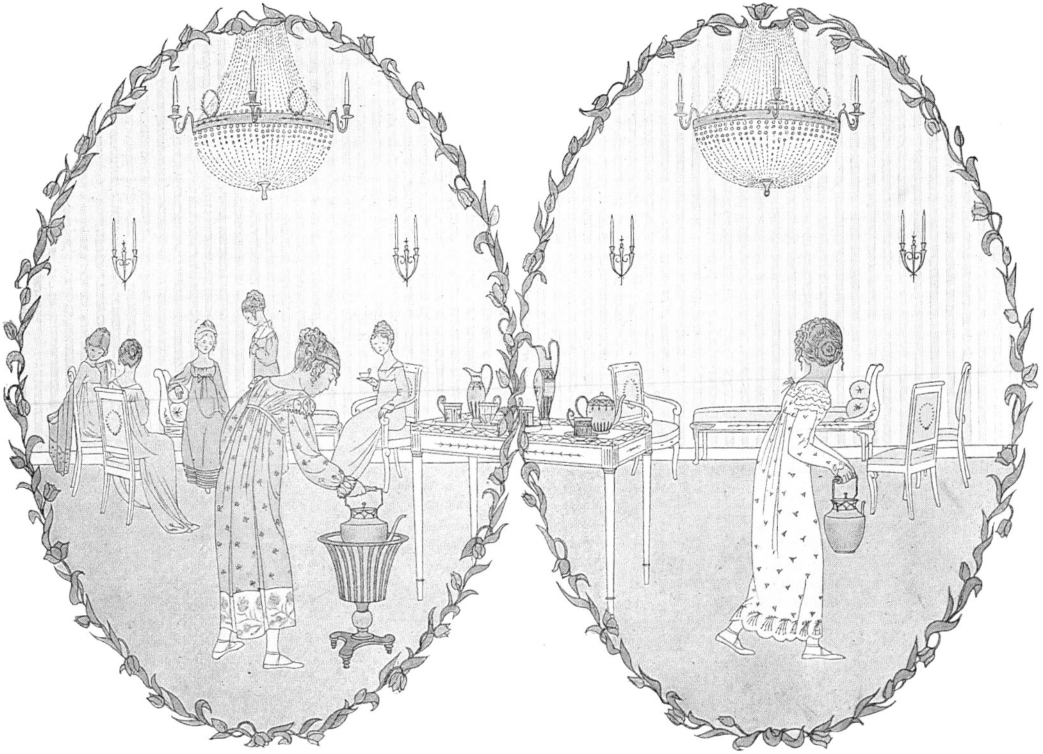

Polly put the kettle on,
Polly put the kettle on,
Polly put the kettle on,
   We'll all have tea.

Sukey take it off again,
Sukey take it off again,
Sukey take it off again,
   They've all gone away.

Hush-a-bye, baby,
On the tree top,
When the wind blows
    The cradle will rock;
When the bough breaks
    The cradle will fall,
Down will come baby,
    Cradle and all.